THE AMAZING ADVENTURES OF THE

DC SUPER-PETS!™

The Marvelous Boxing Bunny

by **Steve Korté**

illustrated by **Mike Kunkel**

PICTURE WINDOW BOOKS
a capstone imprint

Published by Picture Window Books, an imprint of Capstone.
1710 Roe Crest Drive
North Mankato, Minnesota 56003
capstonepub.com

Library of Congress Cataloging-in-Publication Data
Names: Korté, Steven, author. | Kunkel, Mike, 1969– illustrator.
Title: The marvelous boxing bunny / by Steve Korté ; illustrated
by Mike Kunkel.
Description: North Mankato, Minnesota : Picture Window Books, [2022] |
Series: The amazing adventures of the DC super-pets | Audience: Ages 5–7. |
Audience: Grades K–1. | Summary: On a visit to the animal carnival, Hoppy
the bunny has to transform into his superhero identity, Marvel Bunny, to save
his friends from the evil Mr. Mind and Dribodod.
Identifiers: LCCN 2021054286 (print) | LCCN 2021054287 (ebook) |
ISBN 9781666344332 (hardcover) | ISBN 9781666344370 (paperback) |
ISBN 9781666344387 (pdf)
Subjects: LCSH: Rabbits—Juvenile fiction. | Superheroes—Juvenile fiction.
| Supervillains—Juvenile fiction. | CYAC: Rabbits—Fiction. | Superheroes—
Fiction. | Supervillains—Fiction. | LCGFT: Animal fiction. Classification: LCC
PZ7.K8385 Mar 2022 (print) | LCC PZ7.K8385 (ebook) | DDC [E]—dc23
LC record available at https://lccn.loc.gov/2021054286
LC ebook record available at https://lccn.loc.gov/2021054287

Designed by Kay Fraser
Design Elements by Shutterstock/SilverCircle

Printed and bound in the USA. 4882

TABLE OF CONTENTS

He is wise and courageous.
He has amazing superpowers.
He is Shazam's loyal companion.
These are . . .

THE AMAZING
ADVENTURES OF

Hoppy the
Marvel Bunny!

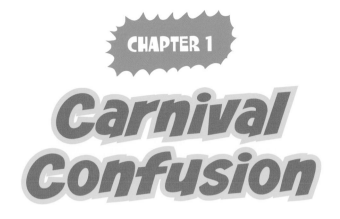

CHAPTER 1

Carnival Confusion

It's a beautiful day in Fawcett City.

Hoppy the rabbit is visiting an animal

carnival with his good friends Millie and

Tawky Tawny. They stop at a tent where

a boxing match is about to take place.

"We're looking for one volunteer!"

calls out a large dog. "The winner of

this fight will win a big cash prize!"

"Hoppy, you should do it!" says

Millie.

"Who, me?" says Hoppy nervously.

"I'd be too afraid of getting hurt!"

Millie doesn't know that Hoppy is secretly a Super Hero. When Hoppy says the magic word "Shazam!," he turns into the superpowered Marvel Bunny.

Hoppy has to make Millie think he is afraid. He starts to back away.

"Ouch!" yells Hoppy as he bumps

into a porcupine's sharp quills.

"Why don't you watch where you're

going?" scolds the porcupine.

Hoppy quickly hops back and

stumbles into the arms of the carnival

dog in front of the boxing tent.

"We have a volunteer!" says the dog

as he drags Hoppy into the tent. "You're

a brave rabbit, my friend!"

CHAPTER 2

Battling Bunny

"Wait, there's been a mistake,"

Hoppy cries. "I'm not a fighter!"

"Don't worry," says the dog. He puts

boxing gloves on Hoppy and tosses him

into the ring. "It'll be over soon!"

Millie and Tawky Tawny join the

audience inside the tent.

Just then, Hoppy's opponent climbs

into the ring. Hoppy sighs with relief.

He sees that he will be fighting his good

friend and favorite Super Hero, Shazam.

DING!

The fight begins. Hoppy smiles and

takes a friendly step toward Shazam.

Hoppy is surprised to see that

Shazam is not smiling back at him.

Shazam draws back his arm. He is
about to throw a punch.

"Yikes!" cries Hoppy as he jumps
back in alarm.

Hoppy bounces off the ropes
surrounding the boxing ring. The
startled rabbit soars through the air
and clear out of the tent!

THUD!

Hoppy crashes to the ground.

HELP! HELP!

Suddenly, he hears cries for help

inside the tent.

"Leapin' lettuce!" says Hoppy. "That

sounds like Millie!"

CHAPTER 3

Shazam!

Hoppy jumps to his feet and says

the magic word "Shazam!"

BLAM!

A bolt of lightning shines above him.

In a flash, Hoppy changes into Marvel

Bunny and rushes to the rescue.

Inside the tent, the boxing ring ropes have magically come to life! They are tying up Millie, Tawky Tawny, and the other audience members.

"Marvel Bunny, help us!" yells Tawky Tawny.

Marvel Bunny looks around. He sees two villains at the back of the tent.

One villain is the wicked worm known as Mr. Mind. He can control the minds of others.

Mr. Mind is sitting on the shoulder of Dribodod, a magical bird from the Fifth Dimension. The only way to send Dribodod back to his realm is to trick him into saying his name backward.

"You're too late, Marvel Bunny," says
Mr. Mind with an evil chuckle. "I used
my mind powers to control Shazam.
And Dribodod used magic to bring the
ropes to life. Dribodod's magic and
my amazing brain are an unbeatable
combination!"

"That's right," agrees Dribodod.

"Mr. Mind and I are perfect partners in crime."

Marvel Bunny reaches into his pocket and removes a piece of paper. He turns his back to the two villains and quickly writes something on it.

"Well, you aren't *equal* partners," says Marvel Bunny as he turns to face them. "This is a contract. It says Mr. Mind is the real head of the team because he is smarter than Dribodod."

"Let me see that!" Dribodod says angrily as he grabs the paper. "Hey! This isn't a contract. It's just a slip of paper with the word Dodobird—"

POOF!

Dribodod has been tricked into reading his name backward. With a puff of smoke, he disappears into the Fifth Dimension. Because Mr. Mind was on Dribodod's shoulder, the tiny worm vanishes too.

The ropes around Millie, Tawky

Tawny, and the other audience

members fall to the ground. Shazam is

no longer controlled by Mr. Mind.

"I'm sorry about trying to hit you!"

Shazam says to Marvel Bunny.

"You saved the day," declares Millie

as she wraps her arms around Marvel

Bunny. "What a shame that Hoppy

missed all the excitement!"

AUTHOR!

Steve Korté is the author of many books for children and young adults. He worked for many years at DC Comics, where he edited more than 600 books about Superman, Batman, Wonder Woman, and the other heroes and villains in the DC Universe. He lives in New York City with his husband, Bill, and their super-cat, Duke.

ILLUSTRATOR!

Mike Kunkel wanted to be a cartoonist ever since he was a little kid. He has worked on numerous projects in animation and books, including many years spent drawing cartoon stories about creatures and super heroes such as the Smurfs and Shazam. He has won the Annie Award for Best Character Design in an Animated Television Production and is the creator of the two-time Eisner Award-winning comic book series Herobear and the Kid. Mike lives in southern California, and he spends most of his extra time drawing cartoons filled with puns, trying to learn new magic tricks, and playing games with his family.

"Word Power"

audience (AW-dee-uhns)—people who watch or listen to a play, movie, or sport

combination (KAHM-buh-nay-shun)—a mixture of two or more things

contract (KAHN-trakt)—a legal agreement

dimension (duh-MEN-shuhn)—a place in space and time

opponent (uh-POH-nuhnt)—a person who competes against another person

realm (RELM)—a world or kingdom

rescue (RESS-kyoo)—to save someone in danger

vanish (VAN-ish)—to disappear

villain (VIL-uhn)—a wicked, evil, or bad person who is often a character in a story

volunteer (vol-uhn-TIHR)—a person who chooses to do work without pay

WRITING PROMPTS

1. Hoppy accidentally volunteers for the boxing match. Write a paragraph about a time you volunteered to do something. Describe how doing so made you feel.

2. Dribodod's name spelled backward is Dodobird. Write your own name backward and then draw a picture of a hero or villain to go with it.

3. At the end of the story, Mr. Mind and Dribodod return to the Fifth Dimension? Write a new chapter that describes what happens when they get there. You decide!

DISCUSSION QUESTIONS

1. Hoppy hides his secret identity as Marvel Bunny from Millie. Why do you think he does that?

2. Dribodod uses his magic to bring the boxing ring ropes to life. What would you bring to life if you had his powers?

3. Who do you think is smarter, Mr. Mind or Marvel Bunny? Explain your answer.

THE AMAZING ADVENTURES OF THE

DC SUPER-PETS!

Collect them all!